Yoram Gross

Blinky Bill ™/®
Leads the Gang

by David and Carol Witt
adapted by Sally Farrell Odgers

an
ABC
BOOK

Illustration by
artists of Yoram Gross Film Studios
based on scenes from the ABC TV series
The Adventures of Blinky Bill

During the school holidays, Blinky Bill and his friends decided to earn some money to build a new club house.

'This is wonderful!' said Nutsy, at the end of the week. 'We've earnt two hundred and fifty gumnuts, three pine cones – and a button.'

'That's a fortune!' cried Splodge excitedly.

Just then, Danny Dingo appeared from behind a tree.

'Did someone say *fortune*?' he asked. 'That's a lot of money. I hope your club's leader will help you spend it wisely.'

'Our club doesn't have a leader!' said Marcia.

'How do we get one?' asked Splodge.

Danny glanced cunningly at the Gang. 'The fairest way is to vote for one. Why not vote for me?'

'No, vote for me!' cried Blinky but Danny was one step ahead of him.

Greenpatch had its share of shady creatures. Amongst them were the Fat Cats and Danny Dingo borrowed money from them to run an exciting election campaign. He promised to give everyone pocket money and to build a swimming pool if he was voted club leader.

'What will you do for the club if *you* win, Blinky?' asked Nutsy.

Blinky hadn't thought about this. He was sure his friends would vote for him.

But later, when the votes were counted, Wombo announced that Danny had won the election.

The first thing Danny did as the leader was to make his brothers and sister his assistants.

'Now, which of my promises will I carry out first?' he asked Daisy, Meatball and Shifty Dingo.

'The swimming pool!' they yelled.

Blinky and his friends were delighted until they found out who was going to do the work. Within minutes, Danny had handed out shovels and wheelbarrows.

'Start digging!' he ordered.

Flap was soon bored with all the hard work. 'Hey Danny! Where's our pocket money?' he demanded.

'You'll get it,' said Danny. 'You have to work for it though!'

Flap, Splodge, Nutsy, Marcia and Blinky worked so hard that the swimming pool was soon ready to use.

As soon as Danny had declared it open, the dingo family raced into the pool.
When Blinky and his friends tried to follow, Danny locked them out!

'Hey!' squeaked Marcia. 'We want a swim, too!'

'This pool is for the club leader and the club leader's friends only,' said Danny.
'If you want to swim, get your own pool.'

'But we can't afford a pool!' protested Nutsy.

'You can if you work harder,' said Daisy Dingo.

'And lucky for you, we have work right here,' added Danny.

So, while the dingoes played in the pool, Blinky and his friends ran back and forth with drinks and suntan cream.

'This club isn't as much fun as it used to be!' puffed Flap.

'It is for us!' called Danny.

One day, the Fat Cats appeared at the pool. 'When are you going to pay us back, Danny?' they demanded. 'We want our money back, right now!'

'Sure thing,' promised Danny.

'But Danny, we don't have the money!' whispered Daisy.

Danny grinned. 'I have a plan,' he sneered.

Danny finally gave Blinky and his friends their pocket money – twenty gumnuts each.
Daisy then stepped in to remind the Gang about taxes, which also just happened
to add up to twenty gumnuts each.

'At least it's all going to the club,' said Splodge with a sigh as he and the others handed back their money.

'We must have enough for a new pool *and* a club house by now!' said Flap.

'Exactly how much money *do* we have Daisy?' asked Nutsy.

'Let's see ... ten thousand gumnuts,' said Daisy.

'The club has ten thousand gumnuts to spend!' cried Blinky.

'No,' corrected Daisy. 'The club *owes* ten thousand gumnuts. Danny borrowed it from the Fat Cats.'

'Now we'll never build the club house!' cried Marcia. 'This is all Danny's fault, but we're the ones who will have to pay the Fat Cats back.'

'No we won't,' said Blinky. 'I have a plan. We can't get Danny out of the club, but what if we leave the club ourselves? Then there'll be nobody for Danny to boss about and he'll have to pay all the money back himself!'

And that's what happened. Blinky and his friends resigned from the club and when the Fat Cats came to collect their money, there was only one thing Danny could do. He handed the swimming pool over to the Fat Cats and went to work for them himself.

Soon, he and the other dingoes were running back and forth with drinks and suntan cream.

'No we won't,' said Blinky. 'I have a plan. We can't get Danny out of the club, but what if we leave the club ourselves? Then there'll be nobody for Danny to boss about and he'll have to pay all the money back himself!'

And that's what happened. Blinky and his friends resigned from the club and when the Fat Cats came to collect their money, there was only one thing Danny could do. He handed the swimming pool over to the Fat Cats and went to work for them himself.

Soon, he and the other dingoes were running back and forth with drinks and suntan cream.